CW00864839

A Note to Parents & Teachers—

Welcome to We Can Readers from Xist Publishing! These books are designed to inspire discovery and delight in the youngest readers. Each short book features very simple sentences with visual cues to get kids reading for the first time.

You can help each child develop a lifetime love of reading right from the very start. Here are some ways to help a beginning reader get going:

- Read the book aloud as a first introduction
- Run your fingers below the words as you read each line
- Give the child the chance to finish the sentences or read repeating words while you read the rest.
- Encourage the child to read aloud every day!

Published proudly in the State of Texas, USA by Xist Publishing
www.xistpublishing.com
24200 Southwest Freeway Suite 402- 290 Rosenberg, TX 77471

eISBN: 978-1-5324-2715-2
Saddle Stitch ISBN: 978-1-5324-2716-9
Perfect Bound ISBN: 978-1-5324-4112-7
Hardcover ISBN: 978-1-5324-3544-7

Nat Can Help

Brenda Ponnay

xist Publishing

Nat likes to help.

He helps his mom
with the trash.

He helps his dad
with the leaves.

He helps his grandma
with the TV.

He helps his teacher with the papers.

He helps his friend with
the door.

Nat likes to help.

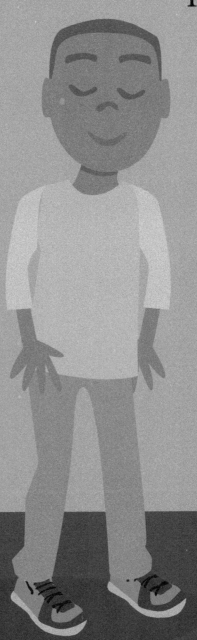

Things to do next!

Write a Sentence

Nat can _____.

Drawing

Draw who you think Nat will help next.

Sharing

Talk to your classmates about how you help other people.

WORD LIST

build	likes
can	mom
dad	Nat
door	papers
friend	teacher
grandma	the
He	think
help	to
helps	trash
his	tv
leaves	with

Have you read all of the

We Can Readers?

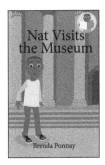

Nat Visits the Museum

Brenda Ponnay

Nat and Raj

Brenda Ponnay

Wet Dog

Brenda Ponnay

Su and Kat

Brenda Ponnay

Su Sees

Brenda Ponnay

Bandit Naps

Brenda Ponnay

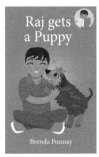

Raj gets a Puppy

Brenda Ponnay

A Bath for Bandit

Brenda Ponnay

Buddy Licks

Brenda Ponnay

Bandit Eats Grass

Brenda Ponnay

Buddy Plays Fetch

Brenda Ponnay

Ready for the Test

Brenda Ponnay

Lemonade Stand

LEMONADE 25¢

Brenda Ponnay

Last Day of School

Brenda Ponnay

Raj Cleans Up

Brenda Ponnay

CPSIA information can be obtained
at www.ICGtesting.com
Printed in the USA
BVHW022208260922
648070BV00004B/12